W9-BMQ-758

Two Strikes Four Eyes

Written and illustrated by NED DELANEY

Houghton Mifflin Company Boston 1976

For Andree, Granny and Not-so-fatso

Also by NED DELANEY
One Dragon to Another

Library of Congress Cataloging in Publication Data

Delaney, Ned.
Two strikes four eyes.

SUMMARY: Afraid that his teammates will tease him, Toby refuses to wear his glasses until he realizes that playing well is more important.
[1. Eyeglasses—Fiction. 2. Baseball—Fiction. 3. Mice—Fiction] I. Title.
PZ7.D3732Tw [E] 76-14348
ISBN 0-395-24744-6

PRINTED IN THE UNITED STATES OF AMERICA.
H 10 9 8 7 6 5 4 3 2 1

Toby was a mouse who loved to play baseball.
He loved everything about the game.
He loved the sound the bat made when it hit the ball,
the roar of the crowd, and even the smell of hot dogs
and peanuts that came from the stands.

But Toby couldn't see beyond the end of his whiskers without his glasses. None of his teammates needed glasses. They were the best rat athletes around. Toby could never let them see him with his glasses on. "I bet they'd call me Sissy or Four Eyes," he thought.

No matter how hard Toby tried, nothing went right. He made spectacular leaps for high line drives and twisted his body like a pretzel after bouncing grounders.

But Toby always seemed to twist when he should have leaped and leap when he should have twisted. He just couldn't see the ball.

His teammates were upset with the way Toby played. They teased him all the time. He only got on the team because Oscar Peppercorn had sprained his throwing arm.

"He's the pits!"

"He can't hit the broad side of a barn!"

"He's got two left feet!"

These were only some of the things they said.

16

One day in an important game with the Hogs, Toby heard the batter connect. He ran back for the ball yelling, "I have it! I have it!" Right into Mr. Woodchuck's apple orchard.
He pegged a ripe McIntosh to the infield as two runs scored.

Toby usually struck out, but today Porker Mulligan was having trouble with his dreaded hog-ball. A wild pitch hit Toby's bat and everyone yelled, "Go for first!" Toby ran as fast as he could but took a wrong turn at first base and bumped right into Old Man Chicken. As Toby helped him pick up his groceries he was tagged out.

Muscles Muffins played next to Toby in center field. Toby thought Muscles was all a baseball player could hope to be. He was the strongest and the loudest member of the team.

"Can you help me to play better, Muscles?" asked Toby.
"Help you, kid!" said Muscles. "You're beyond hope."

The big game with the Fowls was coming up in less than a week. Toby had to do something. He was afraid he would be kicked off the team.

"Maybe if I get myself into top physical shape," he thought, "I won't even need my glasses."

He tried all the exercises he could think of.

He lifted weights. He did push-ups.
He did sit-ups.

He ran laps until he was so tired
he could hardly move.
Nothing seemed to help.

The day of the championship game between the Rodents and the Fowls arrived. Both teams played an outstanding game of baseball. Fortunately for Toby no one hit to right field. It was the ninth inning and the Rodents were ahead 4 to 3, but the Fowls were at bat with one bird on base and two outs.

Fast-wing Slim stepped up to the plate. Lefty threw his mousetrap ball. Slim leaned into the pitch and hit a high pop fly to right field. "Toby," cried the Rodents. "Heads up! Heads up!" Toby made a mighty leap for the ball — and missed. He fell over backward with a CRUNCH. Slim rounded the bases, bringing in two runs to put the Fowls ahead 5 to 4.

Toby pulled his glasses from his pocket. One lens was broken.

"You blockhead. You goof," the Rodents angrily yelled. "You're off the team. Turn in your uniform."

The next Fowl struck out. Toby walked slowly back to the dugout for the last time.

"Well," he thought, "as long as I'm off the team, I may as well watch the game." He put on his glasses.

SCRAMBLE THEIR EGGS
DRINK SKUNK COLA
NOW WITH 12 ESSENTIAL VITAMENS

The Rodents still had a chance. The first Rodent struck out, but the second batter got a base hit. The whole team was counting on Muscles Muffins to save the game.

"Come on, we need a homer!" the Rodents cried.

But before anyone knew it the count was three balls and two strikes.

"Don't worry. I'll slam the ball out of the park," said Muscles as he thumped his bat on the plate. Rhode Island Red wound up and threw the ball. Toby felt the breeze from Muscles' mighty swing. Muscles had struck out.

ELECT
THIS OUTSTANDING CITIZEN

“There goes the game,” the Rodents exclaimed.
“There’s no one left. We may as well let Toby take a last turn at bat.”
Toby stepped up to the plate, squinting through his broken glasses.

Rhode Island Red threw his very best
pitch. There was the ball. Toby could *see* it!
He choked up on the bat and swung with all his might.
There was a resounding THWACK. The ball went
sailing far over the heads of the astonished Fowls.

Toby ran the bases without a mistake, bringing in two runs. The Rodents had won the championship 6 to 5. As he crossed home plate his fellow Rodents cheered.

"Hooray for Toby!"

"Good going, Toby!"

"What a terrific hit!"

"Why didn't you ever wear your glasses before?" his teammates asked.

Toby didn't say a word.

YOUR NEXT
PRESIDENT!

The following day everyone voted Toby the most valuable player of the game.
And as special appreciation, his teammates chipped in to buy him a brand-new pair of glasses.